Peter's Railway
The Four Seasons

by
Christopher Vine

The watercolour illustrations are by John Wardle

Published by
Christopher Vine 2017

Printed by The Amadeus Press
Copyright © 2017 Christopher Vine

ISBN 978-1-9088970-84

Crossacres Farm
Grandpa's House

Yockle
Scho

Yockletts

River Woe

Watermill

Woodland Cottage
Peter's House

The Peter's Railway Series

Most of the books are set in summertime when there are long, hot days, perfect for adventures on the little railway across the farm. However, the railway is there all year round, even if it isn't being used every day.

This book tells the story of life on the railway through one year, from winter to autumn. With all sorts of different activities and fun, each season brings its own character and rhythm of life.

Winter is a time for indoor construction projects. In spring, as it gets warmer, Grandpa and the children are outside preparing the railway for the summer. Then follows autumn: Now what could three children with a small steam train possibly get up to in autumn?...

Winter

The days were short at this time of year and it was cold outside at Crossacres Farm. Snow was lying on the ground in a thick white carpet and the little railway had almost disappeared. The only sign of it were small ridges in the smooth snow - the rails were underneath.

With the animals tucked up in their sheds, Grandpa wasn't very busy on the farm during the winter. The crops and weeds in the fields were dormant, waiting for warmer weather and sunshine to give them energy to grow.

This was not the time of year to be outside playing trains on the railway. However, Peter, Kitty and Harry, still loved helping Grandpa in his workshop.

Grandpa's workshop was a magical place, with all sorts of machines. There was a lathe, a drilling machine, and so many other tools whose use was something of a mystery. It had a unique and lovely smell of old machines, sawdust, smoke and oil.

"Can we help you make something?" Peter asked him one afternoon. "Could we help too?" Kitty and Harry joined in.

"That's an excellent idea," agreed Grandpa with a smile. "And I already have the perfect project for us, it will be really useful too."

The next day, they were all in the workshop and Grandpa had lit the wood-burning stove. It was warm as toast and everyone was very busy working on their latest project - a sleeper painting machine for the railway.

Three years ago, they had spent ages painting all of the wooden sleepers which held the rails together. It wasn't really paint, but a sort of oily wood preservative to stop the sleepers rotting. It had taken them weeks to coat all 50,000 sleepers, and now they needed doing again.

The machine was based on one of their bogie wagons, with a large tank on top. Originally this tank had been a gas cylinder, but now it would hold the special oily paint. A tube from the bottom of the tank took the paint to a pump which forced the paint through some sprayer nozzles.

These spray nozzles were held on a wooden bar, just above the track. They pointed downwards and would be able to paint a sleeper in just a couple of seconds.

The Sleeper Painting Machine

This is the sleeper painting machine which Grandpa and the children have made in the workshop during the winter.

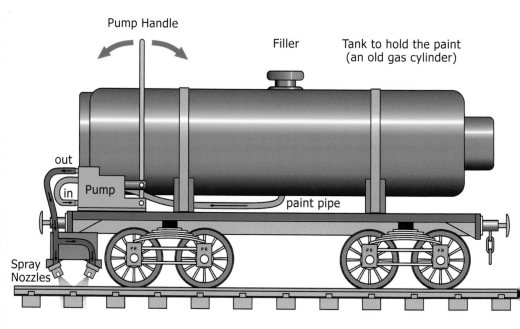

The machine has been constructed from a bogie wagon; an old gas tank to hold the paint; a hand operated pump; and some sprayer nozzles from a farm fertiliser sprayer.

The machine is rolled along the track and positioned so that the spray nozzles are over a sleeper. Then the pump handle is pumped back and forwards once, to spray the paint onto the top and sides of the sleeper.

The pump forces the paint at high pressure through the nozzles to make a fine spray.

The Pump

How does a simple piston pump work?

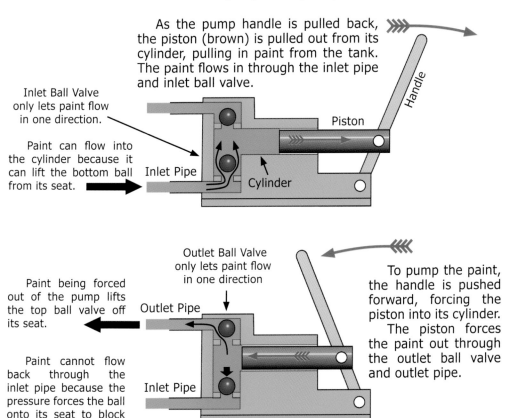

As the pump handle is pulled back, the piston (brown) is pulled out from its cylinder, pulling in paint from the tank. The paint flows in through the inlet pipe and inlet ball valve.

Inlet Ball Valve only lets paint flow in one direction.

Paint can flow into the cylinder because it can lift the bottom ball from its seat.

Inlet Pipe

Piston

Cylinder

Handle

Outlet Ball Valve only lets paint flow in one direction

Paint being forced out of the pump lifts the top ball valve off its seat.

Outlet Pipe

Paint cannot flow back through the inlet pipe because the pressure forces the ball onto its seat to block the flow.

Inlet Pipe

To pump the paint, the handle is pushed forward, forcing the piston into its cylinder.

The piston forces the paint out through the outlet ball valve and outlet pipe.

Spring

The children were at home for the Easter holidays, and it was high time to start sorting out the railway after the ravages of winter.

There was lots to do; painting the stations, clearing leaves and sticks from the track, oiling the points. But first, there was the problem of a huge, old beech tree which had blown down in a storm, completely blocking the line.

Peter, Kitty and Harry were outside, helping Grandpa. He was cutting up the tree while they loaded the logs onto the train.

The scene on the little railway was a hive of activity. They were like busy bees, especially Grandpa, who was buzzing very loudly with his petrol-powered chainsaw!

Next day, with the line now clear of obstructions, they could take a run along the length of the railway. After loading up the train with tools and a picnic, they set off for another day of enjoyable work.

Kitty drove Quicksilver with several train-loads of logs up to the farm, for Grandpa and Grandma to burn next winter. In fact there were so many logs that she drove another few loads down the line to Woodland Cottage for their stove. Mum and Dad stacked them neatly in the log shed and thanked the children for such a good supply of free winter fuel!

Peter and Harry were down at Woodland Cottage too, painting the little station. They had already rubbed down the old, flaky paint with sandpaper and were now brushing on gloss paint. In a few hours the station looked brand new again.

While the boys were busy painting, Grandpa and Kitty started on some proper railway engineering. The winter rain had caused the line to sink in places and they were setting it level again.

Grandpa lifted up the track a little, while Kitty shovelled and raked some fresh ballast stones underneath, to support it. Then they checked it carefully with a spirit level and made a few final adjustments. When it was perfect, they moved on to the next length which had sunk.

It took them two days but, at last, with the track sorted out, it was nearly time to raise steam in Fiery Fox for some high speed running.

But there was still one last job to do: painting all of the 50,000 sleepers. For this they would need their new machine. They wheeled it out.

"I name this machine, *SPLAT*," announced Kitty, regally. "It stands for *Sleeper Painting, Labour-saving, Automatic Train*." Little did she realise, as she proudly painted this on the tank, how accurate the name would be.

They coupled it up to the electric locomotive, Quicksilver. Then, with Kitty driving, Harry directing, and Peter working the pump, the machine sprayed the oily paint brilliantly.

The only trouble was that it sprayed in all directions at once! On the sleepers, on their shoes, socks, trousers... everywhere. Clearly some minor adjustments were necessary.

But they soon got it working correctly and the job was finished in just three days. Much quicker than doing it by hand, and much more fun.

Summer

With the warm weather here at last, the children were enjoying their railway again.

One evening, after a long, hot day of running trains, Grandma had one of her fabulous ideas. "I've been reading about the local children's hospital," she explained. "They need money to buy toys for the sick children to play with. Why don't you organise a sponsored event on the railway? You could raise lots of money to help them."

They all started talking at once, but it was Harry who had the best idea. "Why don't we see how far we could drive a train in one whole day *and* night?" he suggested. "We could ask people to sponsor us, £1 for every circuit of the railway. It would be fantastic fun too!" he grinned.

During the following weeks, the children asked everyone they knew to sponsor them or to buy tickets. They put up posters in the village and even wrote an article for the local newspaper. The great event was set for the first day in August.

Grandpa had everything ready, including a huge pile of coal. "We don't want Fiery Fox to run out in the middle of the night," he laughed.

The children wanted to do all of the driving themselves. "Then it will be all our own work and people will be more generous with their donations," they explained to Grandpa.

"We'll take it in turns," agreed Peter. "We can swap drivers every two hours, and then eat and sleep until it's our next turn of duty. We'll take it in turns to drive, eat and sleep for a solid 24 hours."

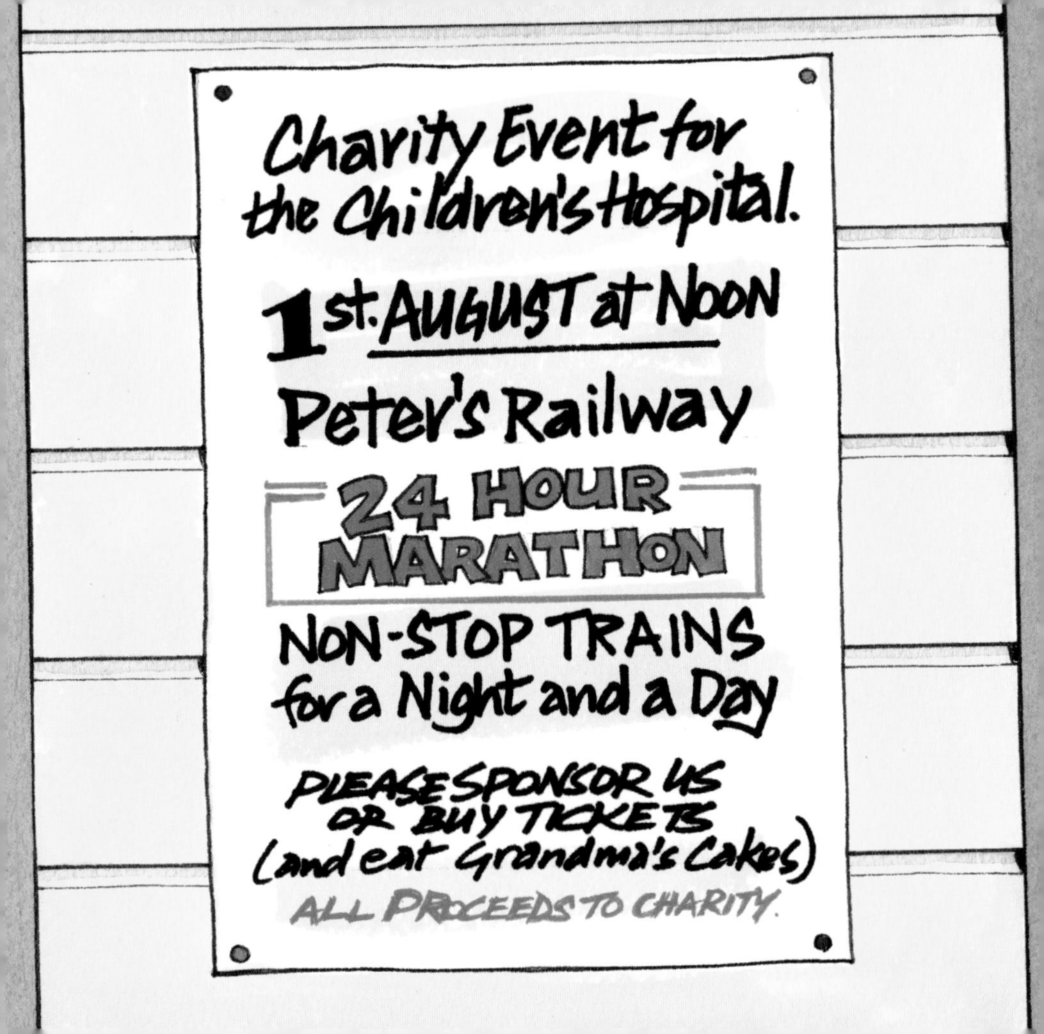
Charity Event for the Children's Hospital.
1st. AUGUST at NOON
Peter's Railway
24 HOUR MARATHON
NON-STOP TRAINS for a Night and a Day
PLEASE SPONSOR US OR BUY TICKETS (and eat Grandma's Cakes)
ALL PROCEEDS TO CHARITY.

On the morning of the big day, the sun was shining and the children were up bright and early. They couldn't wait to get started.

They knew the routine for raising steam in Fiery Fox. Kitty lit the fire, while Harry filled the tender with coal and water, and Peter oiled all the moving parts. By midday, quite a crowd had gathered to watch the proceedings and the train was loaded up with passengers.

"Drive steadily," Grandpa told the children. "High speed might mean more laps, but you could easily have a crash and ruin your chances of raising lots of money. Good Luck!" he added.

Grandpa waved a bright green flag, and Peter, who was doing the first stint, gave a long blast on the whistle and set off down the line.

Peter set up a steady pace and soon worked out how often he needed to put more coal on the fire. Each circuit of the railway was just over two miles long and took around ten minutes. Every four laps he stopped to fill up the tender with coal and water, while Grandpa oiled the engine for him.

By the time the sun went down, they had already completed 40 circuits of the railway. At nightfall the event took on a completely new character. Sparks flew up from Fiery Fox's chimney, and the hot fire lit up the children's faces as they drove through the dark countryside.

Hour after hour, mile after mile they drove. The children were tired, but the excitement, and raising money for the hospital, kept them going through the night. Drive, eat, sleep, repeat...

By the time the village clock struck noon the next day, they had completed an amazing 124 laps.

While Peter and Grandpa dropped the fire and wiped the oil and soot from Fiery Fox, Kitty and Harry were doing some mathematics.

There was a crowd of spectators at the station, and Kitty clapped her hands for attention. "We have driven for 260 miles and raised just over £5000," she announced with delight. "Thank you all for sponsoring us so generously!"

After a loud cheer, everyone turned to a table which was groaning under the weight of pots of tea and tons of Grandma's cakes. They didn't last long!

An hour later, tired but very happy, the children tumbled into bed - exhausted. Now it was time for sleep, sleep and ZZZZzzzzzzzzzzzzzzzzzzzzzzzzzzzzzzz

Autumn

One day in October, with the wind blowing the leaves from the trees, Mr Esmond arrived with his latest locomotive, Duchess of Hamilton. He had come to test it on the railway for the first time.

She was a wonderful model with a huge, streamlined boiler and four cylinders, making her immensely powerful. In her red and gold livery, Duchess of Hamilton looked stunning.

Mr Esmond drove the new locomotive for a few circuits, checking and adjusting things until he was satisfied. "Would you like to drive?" he asked the children. "I know how careful you are."

They all took it in turns to drive and discovered the engine was so powerful that it pulled all their wagons as if they weren't there at all!

"Keep going!" called Mr Esmond from the back of the train. "She needs a bit of running-in, you're doing a grand job for me!"

By the time they stopped, it was getting dark. They dropped the fire, wiped down the locomotive and enjoyed a well-deserved cup of tea in the shed.

"It won't be long before we have to pack up the railway for the winter," Grandpa announced sadly. "It'll soon be rather too cold to play trains."

But Peter had another idea. "Now that the days are getting shorter," he said, "why don't we have an after-dark, spooky train party? It would be fantastic fun."

"Yes! A Ghost Train party!" squealed Harry and Kitty, together. "We could invite all our friends, and make pumpkin lanterns and… and… and…"

"Slow down!" laughed Grandpa. But it was too late, the children had made up their minds.

There were still a few weeks until Halloween, and the children spent every single spare minute converting the railway into a stage-set for the Ghost Train.

Kitty and Harry were busy making pumpkin lanterns in industrial quantities, with Grandma helping them to cut off the tops with a large knife. "Always keep your hand and fingers behind the knife," explained Grandma seriously. "Then if it slips, you won't cut yourself."

They scooped out the insides and cut the shapes for the faces. There were big ones and small ones, some with scary faces and some with toothy grins. One of Harry's looked weirdly like Harry himself!

Peter was busy too, working on a top-secret project. He was upstairs in his bedroom, designing and building an electric ghost.

He had collected all sorts of useful things: An old bed-sheet, a plastic toy skeleton, an electric motor to make it jiggle about, and some flashing red lamps to light up its eyes.

Finally, he managed to find a movement sensor from an old burglar alarm so that his ghost would leap into life whenever anyone went near it. The burglar alarm had several other useful parts, including a powerful, rechargeable battery which would power the ghost for hours.

Peter was going to hang the whole contraption from a tree in Bluebell Wood.

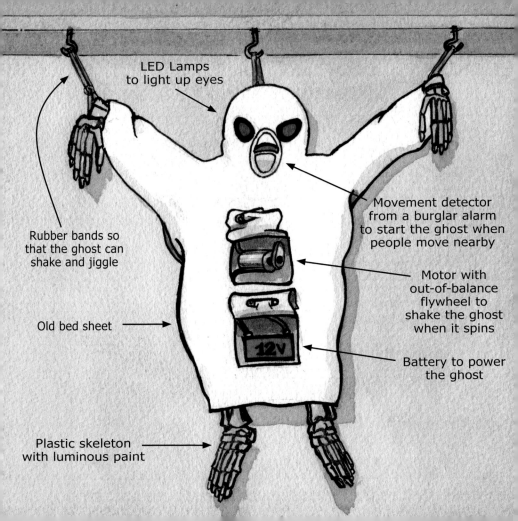

LED Lamps to light up eyes

Rubber bands so that the ghost can shake and jiggle

Old bed sheet

Plastic skeleton with luminous paint

Movement detector from a burglar alarm to start the ghost when people move nearby

Motor with out-of-balance flywheel to shake the ghost when it spins

Battery to power the ghost

12V

The night of the Ghost Train party was crisp and clear, the stars were shining and there was a huge, full moon. All of the children's friends were there, waiting expectantly for the train to depart.

With a mournful blast on the whistle, Peter drove the train slowly out of the little station and off into the night. It was very pretty going across the fields in the moonlight, then they plunged into the pitch-black darkness of Bluebell Wood.

Suddenly they were surrounded by hundreds of ghoulish pumpkins, glowing eerily in the night. It was very scary! Some of the children screamed with glee; some of them screamed with fear.

Moments later, they passed Peter's electric ghost which leapt into life, eyes gleaming, as they shot by. This time, *everyone* screamed!

Later in the evening, they were all enjoying a feast of food and drink when, without warning, a train appeared out of the night. It slid silently through the station.

There were no people on this train, but every single seat was occupied by pumpkins, grinning crazily in the dark. There was no one driving, just a pumpkin in the cab of the engine, staring out ahead.

Everyone was amazed, and the younger children were really frightened. "What's going on?" they all asked. "I don't like it!" whispered one small boy.

"Don't worry," Harry explained to them. "It will be my brother, Peter, playing a trick! He'll be lying down inside the train, out of sight so you can't see him. He's just trying to scare you."

The little children were very relieved to hear this, and the adults were most amused that they had been tricked by young Peter.

But then, just as the train was disappearing off into the darkness, Peter walked out of the engine shed, eating a toffee-apple.

Everyone stared, open-mouthed, at him.

"Good heavens!" exclaimed Peter, laughing at all their shocked faces. "Anyone would have thought you had seen a ghost!"

Maybe they had...

The End.

Why Peter's Railway?

Since a very small boy, Chris has always loved everything mechanical, especially steam engines. The first workshop was in his bedroom where he made an electric go-kart when only 8, followed by a mini-bike powered by the engine from a petrol lawn mower.

He spent many holidays on a friend's farm where there was a miniature railway across a field, and so started a love of making model steam locomotives. The latest is Bongo, 8 feet long and the inspiration for Fiery Fox in the books.

Chris wanted to share his love and knowledge of railways and engineering: Peter's Railway is the result.

Books for children who love trains and engineering

Story

Technical

History

Adventure

The hardback books

The five hardback books tell the charming story of Peter and his Grandpa building and running their steam railway across the farm. At the ends of chapters are special how-it-works pages with simple (but accurate) explanations of what has been happening in the story. In addition, Grandpa tells some wonderful stories from the old days on the railways. Age range 6 - 12 years approx.

A new steam railway is born.

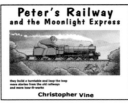

Points, turntables and Peter drives Fiery Fox.

The line is extended and The Great Railway Race.

They build a watermill to power the farm.

Peter helps save the world and makes lots of money!

Activity book with puzzles and colouring - paperback.

Hardback, 96 pages 17 x 24 cm with 30 watercolour pictures by John Wardle and 14 pages of clearly explained technical drawings. £11.99

Paperback books

A series of Peter's Railway in a smaller format. While the original books each contain several story or adventure threads, separate technical pages and Grandpa's tales, the small books concentrate on one aspect; an adventure, a tale from the old railways or a technical book. The four *Little* books are for younger readers.

An adventure on a Scottish holiday which ends with a bang!
Age 6 to 12 years

A true story about an unlucky engine and a brave fireman.
Age 6 to 12 years

A crazy mistake leads to disaster. One of Grandpa's true stories.
Age 6 to 12 years

A cab-ride in a modern diesel and a story from the old days.
Age 6 to 12 years

Our two heroes build a new locomotive from scrap.
Age 6 to 12 years

Grandpa tries to answer a tricky question.
Age 6 to 12 years

The children foil a plot and cause destruction!
Age 6 to 12 years

A storm, getting wet and stealing a train!
Age 6 to 12 years

Peter saves Christmas, a gentle tale.

A bed-time story with a twist...

A railway picnic soon turns into mayhem...

Playing trains on an epic scale!

Little Peter's Railway - Four gentle tales for younger readers, age 3 to 6 years